The GNATS of KNOTTY PINE

BILL PEET

HOUGHTON MIFFLIN COMPANY BOSTON

To my young friends who love toy guns
with the hope that you won't grow up to
love real guns with real bullets that
kill real things.

Manufactured in China

Library of Congress catalog card number: 75-17024

ISBN 0-395-21405-X Reinforced Edition
ISBN 0-395-36612-7 Sandpiper Paperbound Edition

SCP 30 29 28
4500701495

The giant bull moose shivered as he waded up a creek into a ravine. His shivering was not from the chill in the air. The moose was shivering from fright. Tomorrow was the first day of hunting season, which meant terrible trouble for many of the creatures living in Knotty Pine Forest. The big fellow was on his way to a meeting of the animals, held every year on the day before all the shooting began.

When the moose arrived at the meeting place at the end of the ravine a crowd had already gathered. Some were seated on boulders and logs, while others perched on tree limbs.

The purpose of the meeting was to try to figure out some plan to foil the hunters and save their own skins.

An old brown bear was the first to speak and he started things off on a sour note.

"These meetings are a waste of time," he grumbled. "We all know the hunters are out after deer, a prize buck with a fancy pair of antlers. Let the deer worry."

"But if they don't get one of us," protested a big buck, "then they'll shoot at anything on four legs."

"Or on two legs," wailed a quail, "or anything that moves."

"That's right," said a porcupine. "We are all in danger. Hunters kill just for the fun of it. To them it's a game; they like to call it sport."

"I had the wildest dream last night," said a squirrel. "I dreamed that I had a high-powered rifle and two hunters came along without their guns. When I took aim at them they dropped to their knees crying, 'Please! Please! Please don't shoot!! It's not fair!! We don't have our guns. It's not fair! *Please*!'"

"Did you let 'em have it?" asked a bobcat.

"No," said the squirrel. "But I sure gave 'em a bad time. 'Look fellows,' I said, 'no need to get upset. This is only a little ole game, a real fun sport. It wouldn't be much of a sport if your side always

won, would it? Now it's your turn to lose for a change. So cheer
up, my friends.' I kept teasing the hunters until I had them in tears,
then I woke up laughing."

"A lousy dream," snarled the bobcat. "Real dumb!"

"Hold it," said a fat possum. "We can't go on bickering like this. We must all stick together. I say it's all for one and one for all."

"You mean all for nothing," sneered a fox. "We all stick together, then get popped off all in one bunch. Real smart!"

"I've got an idea," said a jack rabbit. "We all take off at once running around and around in all directions and all over the place until the hunters get so dizzy and mixed up they can't shoot straight."

"Ho! Ho!" laughed the fox. "That's great! We run and run until we're all out of breath and fall on our faces. Then the hunters knock us off in their own good time. Just great!"

"O.K.," said the rabbit, "if you're so smart let's hear *your* plan. I'm all ears."

"I say we all do our own thing," said the fox. "The runners run, the climbers climb, and the hiders hide, just as we always have."

"I hate to agree with a smart alec," said the moose, "but I do believe the fox is right. We have no other choice."

After that no one could think of a thing to say and the crowd settled into a deep silence.

At this point a swarm of gnats joined the meeting, and the top gnat, known as Nate, came buzzing up alongside the moose, right up to his ear.

"Do you mind," said Nate, "if I have a few words, sir?"

"Speak up," said the moose, "but make it short. This is no time for small talk."

Nate shouted at the top of his voice to make sure all could hear. "We gnats of Knotty Pine Forest have been thinking!"

"Gnats? Thinking?" snickered the fox. "Now I've heard everything."

"When a billion gnats get their heads together," shouted Nate, "it adds up to one big brain! With *big* ideas!!! We have thought of a plan to save you from the hunters!"

"Goody! Goody!" chortled the fox. "Our worries are over."

"Not funny," growled the bear. "Gnats drive me bats."

"Me, too," grumped the moose. "Beat it, gnats! Scram! Buzz off! All of you!" And with an angry snort he blasted them out of sight.

After the gnats had gone there was another long silence. By this
time it was nearly sunset and deep shadows crept down the ravine.
Finally the moose said, "We don't seem to be getting anywhere, so
why don't we call it a day?"

Then the meeting broke up and all the unhappy animals went their separate ways. As they left, a squirrel called out from a pine tree, "See you tomorrow, everybody!"

"Maybe so," muttered the moose, "and maybe not."

At dawn the next day the roaring of motors echoed through the trees as jeeps, campers, and pick-up trucks came up the road below the forest. Then came the voices of the hunters laughing and shouting as they hauled out their guns.

Up in the forest, panic set in. The deer, the fox and the rabbits raced off in all directions. The quail hid under bushes, and the porcupines and skunks crawled into hollow logs.

The bobcats, raccoons, possums, chipmunks and squirrels crowded into the treetops.

The bears scrambled into a dense tangle of brush, and so did the moose. But alas, he left his great pair of antlers in full view.

While the animals were all in a wild-eyed frenzy, the hunters were as calm as could be, and ever so quiet. They knew that wild things have good ears, and hoped to catch them by surprise. This was the first rule of the game, and as the men headed up the slope toward the forest they walked very softly and talked in whispers with their rifles all set for a shot. They were just a few yards away from the first clump of trees when all of a sudden —

out of the grass swarmed great clouds of gnats! Billions of them!
And leading each cloud was a fearless flight commander shouting
orders, "Go for their heads! Go for their faces! Go for their eyes!
Buzz 'em! Buzz 'em! Drive 'em bats!! Go gnats! Go gnats! Go!
Go! Go!!"

Now the hunters were the ones caught by surprise. The gnat attack
was so sudden and so blinding the hunters were sent staggering back
on their heels.

"What in blazes is this?" one of them yelled.

"Gnats! You knot head," yelled another. "Gnats! Billions of them! The pesky little devils! They're driving me bats!"

In seconds every last man was caught with his head in a great buzzing cloud of gnats. The hunters flew into a rage swatting and slapping wildly at the storm of tiny insects. Some swung away with their rifles hitting nothing but thin air.

One rifle went off *KER–BAM* barely missing one of the men. That did it. "Let's get outta here!" someone shouted, "before we all get killed!"

"Which way is out?" shouted another.

"Downhill, you dope!" and the battle was over. The hunters dropped their rifles and fled down the hill to their campers, jeeps and pick-ups. And with a great roaring of motors they took off.

As the last Jeep disappeared into the distance the gnats formed a big "V" for victory, then let go with a rousing cheer that could be heard for at least twenty feet. The victory was especially sweet since it was won without bloodshed. Not one single gnat was lost.

Now, all the creatures in the forest were deeply indebted to the gnats. Yet there was no way to thank a billion tiny insects scattered all over the forest one by one. So the big bull moose was called upon to thank them all at once.

First he waded out into a stream, since he knew that sound carries better over the water. Then with all his great lungpower the big moose cut loose. "Calling all gnats! Calling all gnats!" he bellowed. "Hear this! Hear this! Thanks a billion!"

The big "THANKS" echoed for miles across the forest and every single gnat heard it loud and clear. Of course this made Nate and his buzzing billions feel mighty big. And from that day on whenever the roar of motors echoed through Knotty Pine Forest the gnats took to the air to meet the enemy head on. To them it was a real fun game. Great sport!